Don't Forget
I Love You

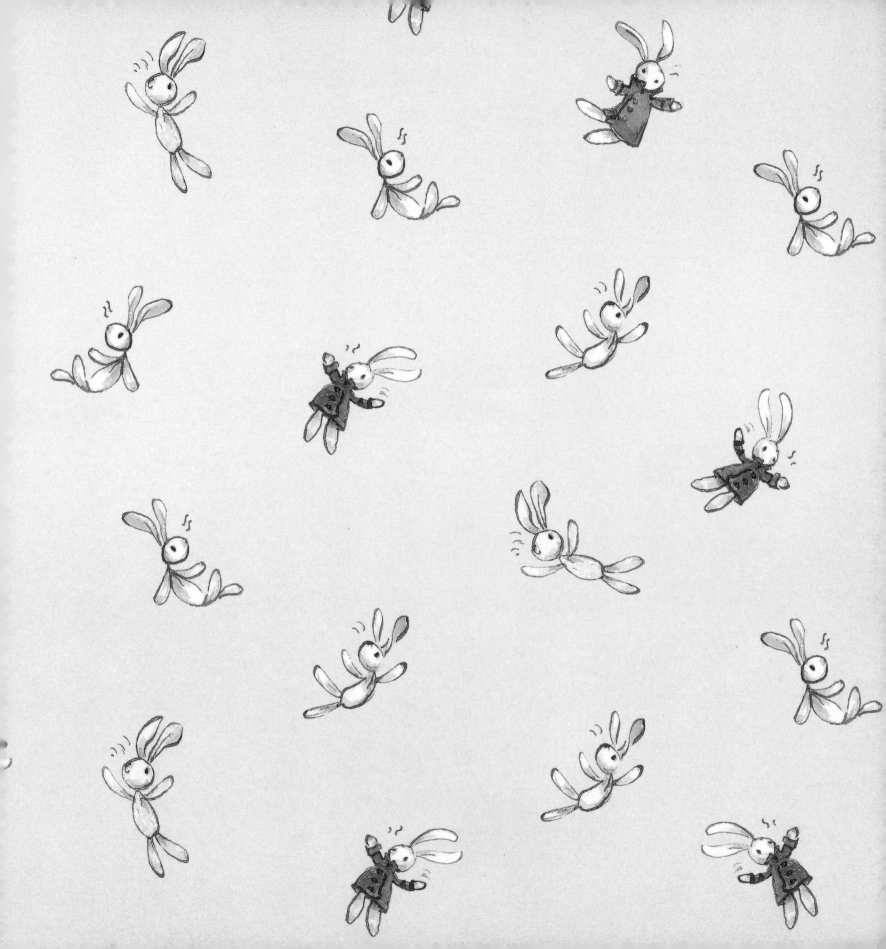

For Imogen, Morwenna, and Finn—M.M.

For Jack and Kerenza—A.C.

PUFFIN BOOKS
Published by the Penguin Group
Penguin Young Readers Group, 345 Hudson Street, New York, New York 10014, U.S.A.
Penguin Group (Canada), 90 Eglinton Avenue East, Suite 700, Toronto, Ontario, Canada M4P 2Y3 (a division of Pearson Penguin Canada Inc.)
Penguin Books Ltd, 80 Strand, London WC2R 0RL, England
Penguin Ireland, 25 St Stephen's Green, Dublin 2, Ireland (a division of Penguin Books Ltd)
Penguin Group (Australia), 250 Camberwell Road, Camberwell, Victoria 3124, Australia (a division of Pearson Australia Group Pty Ltd)
Penguin Books India Pvt Ltd, 11 Community Centre, Panchsheel Park, New Delhi - 110 017, India
Penguin Group (NZ), Cnr Airborne and Rosedale Roads, Albany, Auckland 1310,
New Zealand (a division of Pearson New Zealand Ltd)
Penguin Books (South Africa) (Pty) Ltd, 24 Sturdee Avenue, Rosebank, Johannesburg 2196, South Africa

Registered Offices: Penguin Books Ltd, 80 Strand, London WC2R 0RL, England

Originally published in Great Britian by Macmillan Children's Books
First published in the United States of America by Dial Books for Young Readers, a division of Penguin Young Readers Group, 2004
Published by Puffin Books, a division of Penguin Young Readers Group, 2006

5 7 9 10 8 6 4
Text copyright © Miriam Moss, 2004
Illustrations copyright © Anna Currey, 2004
All rights reserved

THE LIBRARY OF CONGRESS HAS CATALOGED THE DIAL EDITION AS FOLLOWS:
Moss, Miriam.
Don't forget I love you / Miriam Moss ; illustrated by Anna Currey.
p.   cm.
Summary: After spending too much time playing with his favorite toy, Billy and his mother are very late
for nursery school and his mother forgets some crucial things as she rushes to work.
ISBN: 0-8037-2920-0
[1. Mother and child—Fiction. 2. Bears—Fiction.]
I. Currey, Anna, ill. II. Title.
PZ7.M85353 Do 2003 [E]—dc21
2002152119

Puffin Books ISBN 0-14-240548-5

Manufactured in China

Don't Forget I Love You

MIRIAM MOSS

Illustrated by ANNA CURREY

PUFFIN BOOKS

When Billy woke up, Rabbit was hiding
down the side of his bed.
"Don't think I can't see you there, Rabbit,"
said Billy, tugging at Rabbit's paw.

"Time for breakfast,"
Mama called from downstairs.
"In a minute," shouted Billy.
"Rabbit's being naughty."

"Come and wash
your sticky paws,"
called Mama.

"In a minute," said Billy.
"Rabbit won't eat his egg.
Hurry up, Rabbit!"

Billy and Rabbit went upstairs to get dressed.

Mama popped her head around the door.

"Get dressed, Billy," she said.

"In a minute," said Billy.

"I think Rabbit's got
a tummy ache."

"Come and brush your teeth, Billy," Mama called.

"In a minute," said Billy.
"Rabbit's buttons are all wrong."
"Get ready first, Billy,
then play with Rabbit," said Mama.

"Ready at last!" said Mama. "But where did I put your boots?"

"They're on my feet," laughed Billy.

"Oh, good." Mama smiled. "Here's your coat. Come on.
We really must go or we'll be late!"

But Billy dashed upstairs.

"Just a minute!" he called.

"Rabbit hasn't said good-bye to the others."

On the way to nursery school, Billy balanced Rabbit and his lunch box on his head. "Be careful," said Mama.
"I am," said Billy, "except Rabbit won't sit still."

Suddenly, Billy's lunch box hit the ground and burst open.

"Oh, Billy!" said Mama crossly.
"Now we really will be late.

Give Rabbit to me and let's get a move on."

But they were very late and had to
run the rest of the way to school.

"Ah, there you are," said Mrs. Brown. "We wondered where you were."
"Sorry," panted Mama. "I have to go, I'm late for work already. Bye, Billy."
And she hurried away.

Billy hung his coat up. "Is something the matter, Billy?" asked Mrs. Brown. "Mama didn't say *I love you*," said Billy. "She always says *I love you*."

"Well, she was in a bit of a hurry,"
said Mrs. Brown.
    "Have you left Rabbit by your coat?
He'll make you feel better."

They looked in Billy's pockets and even in his lunch box.

But Rabbit was nowhere to be found.

"You must have left him at home," said Mrs. Brown.

"But I didn't," said Billy, starting to cry. "I dropped my
lunch box and we had to run and now Rabbit's lost and
I want my mama."

At that moment the door flew open.
It was Mama!
"Oh Billy, I'm so sorry," she cried.
"I forgot to give Rabbit back to you, and
I forgot something else, too . . .

I forgot to say *I love you*."

Billy climbed onto Mama's lap and gently she dried his tears.

"I love you, too," said Billy.
And they gave each other
a big, big hug.

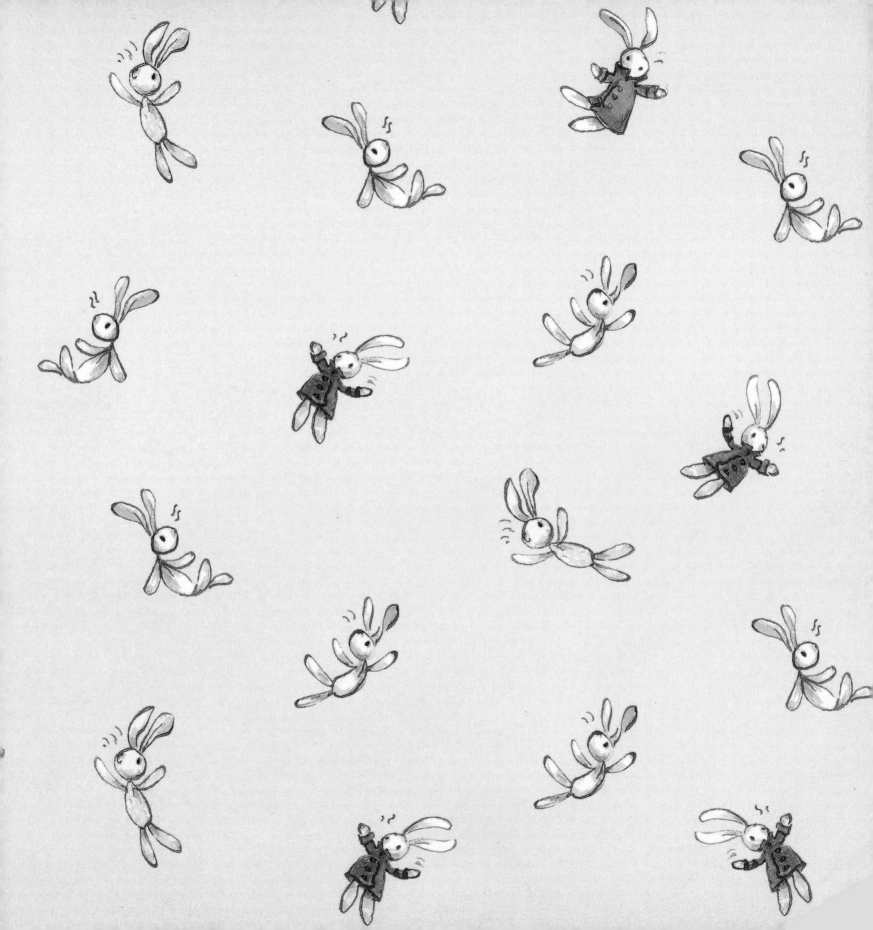